THE DEVIL'S THRONE

In Part 1, Stephen King introduced us to Cold Mountain Penitentiary, and to the lonely stretch of cells known as the Green Mile. There we met Paul Edgecombe, a prison guard assigned to watch over the inmates of Death Row. With the arrival of John Coffey, a hulking man convicted of killing two little girls, the cast of the condemned was completed.

In Part 2, we met the other convicts, Eduard Delacroix and William "Billy the Kid" Wharton, who, along with Coffey, filled out a twisted triangle of death. But the Green Mile began to change when a lonely, squeaky mouse gnawed through barriers between guard and inmate to bring them together, a glowing sense of wonder that warmed even this chill place.

In Part 3, the mystery of the seemingly monstrous John Coffey deepened, as the huge hands of this mountain of a man turned out to have the power to produce uncanny miracles as well as commit unholy murder. What was the strange secret concealed behind his conviction as an unspeakable killer?

Now prepare yourself for the next spine-tingling chapter. . . .

The Green Mile:
Part 4
The Bad Death
of Eduard Delacroix

STEPHEN KING

The Green Mile

PART FOUR

The Bad Death of Eduard Delacroix

A SIGNET BOOK

SIGNET
Published by the Penguin Group
Penguin Books USA Inc., 375 Hudson Street,
New York, New York 10014, U.S.A.
Penguin Books Ltd, 27 Wrights Lane, London W8 5TZ, England
Penguin Books Australia Ltd, Ringwood, Victoria, Australia
Penguin Books Canada Ltd, 10 Alcorn Avenue,
Toronto, Ontario, Canada M4V 3B2
Penguin Books (N.Z.) Ltd, 182–190 Wairau Road,
Auckland 10, New Zealand

Penguin Books Ltd, Registered Offices:
Harmondsworth, Middlesex, England

First published by Signet, an imprint of Dutton Signet,
a division of Penguin Books USA Inc.

First Printing, June, 1996
10 9 8 7 6 5 4 3 2 1

Copyright © Stephen King, 1996
Illustration copyright © Mark Geyer, 1996
Cover art by Robert Hunt
All rights reserved

1

All this other writing aside, I've kept a little diary since I took up residence at Georgia Pines—no big deal, just a couple of paragraphs a day, mostly about the weather—and I looked back through it last evening. I wanted to see just how long it has been since my grandchildren, Christopher and Danielle, more or less forced me into Georgia Pines. "For your own good, Gramps," they said. Of course they did. Isn't that what people mostly say when they have finally figured out how to get rid of a problem that walks and talks?

It's been a little over two years. The eerie thing is that I don't know if it *feels* like two years, or longer than that, or shorter. My sense of time seems to be *melting*, like a kid's snowman in a January thaw. It's as if time as it always was—Eastern Standard Time, Daylight Saving Time, Working-Man Time—doesn't exist anymore. Here there is only Georgia Pines Time, which is Old Man Time, Old Lady Time, and Piss the Bed Time. The rest ... all gone.

This is a dangerous damned place. You don't

realize it at first, at first you think it's only a boring place, about as dangerous as a nursery school at naptime, but it's dangerous, all right. I've seen a lot of people slide into senility since I came here, and sometimes they do more than slide—sometimes they go down with the speed of a crash-diving submarine. They come here mostly all right—dim-eyed and welded to the cane, maybe a little loose in the bladder, but otherwise okay—and then something happens to them. A month later they're just sitting in the TV room, staring up at Oprah Winfrey on the TV with dull eyes, a slack jaw, and a forgotten glass of orange juice tilted and dribbling in one hand. A month after that, you have to tell them their kids' names when the kids come to visit. And a month after that, it's their own damned names you have to refresh them on. Something happens to them, all right: Georgia Pines Time happens to them. Time here is like a weak acid that erases first memory and then the desire to go on living.

You have to fight it. That's what I tell Elaine Connelly, my special friend. It's gotten better for me since I started writing about what happened to me in 1932, the year John Coffey came on the Green Mile. Some of the memories are awful, but I can feel them sharpening my mind and my awareness the way a knife sharpens a pencil, and that makes the pain worthwhile. Writing and memory alone aren't enough, though. I also have a body, wasted and grotesque, though it may now be, and I exercise it as much as I can. It was hard at first—old fogies like me aren't much shakes when it comes to exercise just for the sake of exercise—but it's easier now that there's a purpose to my walks.

I go out before breakfast—as soon as it's light, most days—for my first stroll. It was raining this morning, and the damp makes my joints ache, but I hooked a poncho from the rack by the kitchen door and went out, anyway. When a man has a chore, he has to do it, and if it hurts, too bad. Besides, there are compensations. The chief one is keeping that sense of Real Time, as opposed to Georgia Pines Time. And I like the rain, aches or no aches. Especially in the early morning, when the day is young and seems full of possibilities, even to a washed-up old boy like me.

I went through the kitchen, stopping to beg two slices of toast from one of the sleepy-eyed cooks, and then went out. I crossed the croquet course, then the weedy little putting green. Beyond that is a small stand of woods, with a narrow path winding through it and a couple of sheds, no longer used and mouldering away quietly, along the way. I walked down this path slowly, listening to the sleek and secret patter of the rain in the pines, chewing away at a piece of toast with my few remaining teeth. My legs ached, but it was a low ache, manageable. Mostly I felt pretty well. I drew the moist gray air as deep as I could, taking it in like food.

And when I got to the second of those old sheds, I went in for awhile, and I took care of my business there.

When I walked back up the path twenty minutes

later, I could feel a worm of hunger stirring in my belly, and thought I could eat something a little more substantial than toast. A dish of oatmeal, perhaps even a scrambled egg with a sausage on the side. I love sausage, always have, but if I eat more than one these days, I'm apt to get the squitters. One would be safe enough, though. Then, with my belly full and with the damp air still perking up my brain (or so I hoped), I would go up to the solarium and write about the execution of Eduard Delacroix. I would do it as fast as I could, so as not to lose my courage.

It was Mr. Jingles I was thinking about as I crossed the croquet course to the kitchen door—how Percy Wetmore had stamped on him and broken his back, and how Delacroix had screamed when he realized what his enemy had done—and I didn't see Brad Dolan standing there, half-hidden by the Dumpster, until he reached out and grabbed my wrist.

"Out for a little stroll, Paulie?" he asked.

I jerked back from him, yanking my wrist out of his hand. Some of it was just being startled—anyone will jerk when they're startled—but that wasn't all of it. I'd been thinking about Percy Wetmore, remember, and it's Percy that Brad always reminds me of. Some of it's how Brad always goes around with a paperback stuffed into his pocket (with Percy it was always a men's adventure magazine; with Brad it's books of jokes that are only funny if you're stupid and mean-hearted), some of it's how he acts like he's King Shit of Turd Mountain, but mostly it's that he's sneaky, and he likes to hurt.

He'd just gotten to work, I saw, hadn't even changed into his orderly's whites yet. He was wearing jeans and a cheesy-looking Western-style shirt. In one hand was the remains of a Danish he'd hooked out of the kitchen. He'd been standing under the eave, eating it where he wouldn't get wet. And where he could watch for me, I'm pretty sure of that now. I'm pretty sure of something else, as well: I'll have to watch out for Mr. Brad Dolan. He doesn't like me much. I don't know why, but I never knew why Percy Wetmore didn't like Delacroix, either. And *dislike* is really too weak a word. Percy hated Del's guts from the very first moment the little Frenchman came onto the Green Mile.

"What's with this poncho you got on, Paulie?" he asked, flicking the collar. "This isn't yours."

"I got it in the hall outside the kitchen," I said. I hate it when he calls me Paulie, and I think he knows it, but I was damned if I'd give him the satisfaction of seeing it. "There's a whole row of them. I'm not hurting it any, would you say? Rain's what it's made for, after all."

"But it wasn't made for *you*, Paulie," he said, giving it another little flick. "That's the thing. Those slickers're for the employees, not the residents."

"I still don't see what harm it does."

He gave me a thin little smile. "It's not about *harm*, it's about the *rules*. What would life be without rules? Paulie, Paulie, Paulie." He shook his head, as if just looking at me made him feel sorry to be alive. "You probably think an old fart like you doesn't have to mind about the rules anymore, but that's just not true. *Paulie.*"

Smiling at me. Disliking me. Maybe even hating me. And why? I don't know. Sometimes there *is* no why. That's the scary part.

"Well, I'm sorry if I broke the rules," I said. It came out sounding whiney, a little shrill, and I hated myself for sounding that way, but I'm old, and old people whine easily. Old people *scare* easily.

Brad nodded. "Apology accepted. Now go hang that back up. You got no business out walking in the rain, anyway. Specially not in those woods. What if you were to slip and fall and break your damned hip? Huh? Who do you think'd have to hoss your elderly freight back up the hill?"

"I don't know," I said. I just wanted to get away from him. The more I listened to him, the more he sounded like Percy. William Wharton, the crazyman who came to the Green Mile in the fall of '32, once grabbed Percy and scared him so bad that Percy squirted in his pants. *You talk about this to anyone,* Percy told the rest of us afterward, *and you'll all be on the breadlines in a week.* Now, these many years later, I could almost hear Brad Dolan saying those same words, in that same tone of voice. It's as if, by writing about those old times, I have unlocked some unspeakable door that connects the past to the present—Percy Wetmore to Brad Dolan, Janice Edgecombe to Elaine Connelly, Cold Mountain Penitentiary to the Georgia Pines old folks' home. And if that thought doesn't keep me awake tonight, I guess nothing will.

I made as if to go in through the kitchen door and Brad grabbed me by the wrist again. I don't know about the first one, but this time he was doing it on purpose, squeezing to hurt. His eyes shifting back and forth, making sure no one was around in the early-morning wet, no one to see he was abusing one of the old folks he was supposed to be taking care of.

"What do you do down that path?" he asked. "I know you don't go down there and jerk off, those days are long behind you, so what do you do?"

"Nothing," I said, telling myself to be calm, not to show him how bad he was hurting me and to be calm, to remember he'd only mentioned the path, he didn't know about the shed. "I just walk. To clear my mind."

"Too late for that, Paulie, your mind's never gonna be clear again." He squeezed my thin old man's wrist again, grinding the brittle bones, eyes continually shifting from side to side, wanting to make sure he was safe. Brad wasn't afraid of breaking the rules; he was only afraid of being *caught* breaking them. And in that, too, he was like Percy Wetmore, who would never let you forget he was the governor's nephew. "Old as you are, it's a miracle you can remember *who* you are. You're *too* goddam old. Even for a museum like this. You give me the fucking creeps, Paulie."

"Let go of me," I said, trying to keep the whine out of my voice. It wasn't just pride, either. I thought if he heard it, it might inflame him, the way the smell of sweat can sometimes inflame a bad-tempered dog—one which would otherwise only growl—to bite. That made me think of a reporter who'd covered John Coffey's trial. The reporter was a terrible man named Hammersmith, and the most terrible thing about him was that he hadn't known he was terrible.

Instead of letting go, Dolan squeezed my wrist again. I groaned. I didn't want to, but I couldn't help it. It hurt all the way down to my ankles.

"What do you do down there, Paulie? Tell me."

"Nothing!" I said. I wasn't crying, not yet, but I was afraid I'd start soon if he kept bearing down like that. "Nothing, I just walk, I like to walk, let go of me!"

He did, but only long enough so he could grab my other hand. That one was rolled closed. "Open up," he said. "Let Poppa see."

I did, and he grunted with disgust. It was nothing but the remains of my second piece of toast. I'd clenched it in my right hand when he started squeezing my left wrist, and there was butter—well, oleo, they don't have real butter here, of course—on my fingers.

"Go on inside and wash your damned hands," he said, stepping back and taking another bite of his Danish. "Jesus Christ."

I went up the steps. My legs were shaking, my heart pounding like an engine with leaky valves and shaky old pistons. As I grasped the knob that would let me into the kitchen—and safety—Dolan said: "If

you tell anyone I squeezed your po' old wrist, Paulie,
I'll tell them you're having delusions. Onset of senile
dementia, likely. And you know they'll believe me. If
there are bruises, they'll think you made them yourself."

Yes. Those things were true. And once again, it
could have been Percy Wetmore saying them, a Percy
that had somehow stayed young and mean while I'd
grown old and brittle.

"I'm not going to say anything to anyone," I mut-
tered. "Got nothing to say."

"That's right, you old sweetie." His voice light and
mocking, the voice of a lugoon (to use Percy's word)
who thought he was going to be young forever. "And
I'm going to find out what you're up to. I'm going to
make it my business. You hear?"

I heard, all right, but wouldn't give him the satisfaction of saying so. I went in, passed through the
kitchen (I could now smell eggs and sausage cooking, but no longer wanted any), and hung the poncho
back up on its hook. Then I went upstairs to my
room—resting at every step, giving my heart time to
slow—and gathered my writing materials together.

I went down to the solarium and was just sitting at
the little table by the windows when my friend
Elaine poked her head in. She looked tired, and, I
thought, unwell. She'd combed her hair out but was
still in her robe. We old sweeties don't stand much
on ceremony; for the most part, we can't afford to.

"I won't disturb you," she said, "I see you're getting set to write—"

"Don't be silly," I said. "I've got more time than Carter's got liver pills. Come on in."

She did, but stood by the door. "It's just that I couldn't sleep—again—and happened to be looking out my window a little earlier ... and ..."

"And you saw Mr. Dolan and me having our pleasant little chat," I said. I hoped seeing was all she'd done; that her window had been closed and she hadn't heard me whining to be let go.

"It didn't look pleasant and it didn't look friendly," she said. "Paul, that Mr. Dolan's been asking around about you. He asked *me* about you—last week, this was. I didn't think much about it then, just that he's got himself a nasty long nose for other people's business, but now I wonder."

"Asking about me?" I hoped I didn't sound as uneasy as I felt. "Asking what?"

"Where you go walking, for one thing. And *why* you go walking."

I tried to laugh. "There's a man who doesn't believe in exercise, that much is clear."

"He thinks you've got a secret." She paused. "So do I."

I opened my mouth—to say what, I don't know—but Elaine raised one of her gnarled but oddly beautiful hands before I could get a single word out. "If you do, I don't want to know what it is, Paul. Your business is your business. I was raised to think that way, but not everyone was. Be careful. That's all I want to tell you. And now I'll let you alone to do your work."

She turned to go, but before she could get out the door, I called her name. She turned back, eyes questioning.

"When I finish what I'm writing—" I began, then shook my head a little. That was wrong. "*If* I finish what I'm writing, would you read it?"

She seemed to consider, then gave me the sort of smile a man could easily fall in love with, even a man as old as me. "That would be my honor."

"You'd better wait until you read it before you talk about honor," I said, and it was Delacroix's death I was thinking of.

"I'll read it, though," she said. "Every word. I promise. But you have to finish writing it, first."

She left me to it, but it was a long time before I wrote anything. I sat staring out the windows for almost an hour, tapping my pen against the side of the table, watching the gray day brighten a little at a time, thinking about Brad Dolan, who calls me Paulie and never tires of jokes about chinks and slopes and spicks and micks, thinking about what Elaine Connelly had said. *He thinks you've got a secret. So do I.*

And maybe I do. Yes, maybe I do. And of course Brad Dolan wants it. Not because he thinks it's important (and it's not, I guess, except to me), but because he doesn't think very old men like myself should have secrets. No taking the ponchos off the hook outside the kitchen; no secrets, either. No getting the idea that the likes of us are still human. And why shouldn't we be allowed such an idea? He doesn't know. And in that, too, he is like Percy.

So my thoughts, like a river that takes an oxbow turn, finally led back to where they had been when Brad Dolan reached out from beneath the kitchen eave and grabbed my wrist: to Percy, mean-spirited Percy Wetmore, and how he had taken his revenge on the man who had laughed at him. Delacroix had been throwing the colored spool he had—the one Mr. Jingles would fetch—and it bounced out of the cell and into the corridor. That was all it took; Percy saw his chance.

2

"*No, you fool!*" Brutal yelled, but Percy paid no attention. Just as Mr. Jingles reached the spool—too intent on it to realize his old enemy was at hand—Percy brought the sole of one hard black workshoe down on him. There was an audible snap as Mr. Jingles's back broke, and blood gushed from his mouth. His tiny black eyes bulged in their sockets, and in them I read an expression of surprised agony that was all too human.

Delacroix screamed with horror and grief. He threw himself at the door of his cell and thrust his arms out through the bars, reaching as far as he could, crying the mouse's name over and over.

Percy turned toward him, smiling. Toward me and Brutal, as well. "There," he said. "I knew I'd get him, sooner or later. Just a matter of time, really." He turned and walked back up the Green Mile, leaving Mr. Jingles lying on the linoleum, his spreading blood red over green.

Dean got up from the duty desk, hitting the side of it with his knee and knocking the cribbage board to the floor. The pegs spilled out of their holes and rolled in all directions. Neither Dean nor Harry, who had been just about to go out, paid the slightest attention to the overturn of the game. "What'd you do this time?" Dean shouted at Percy. "What the hell'd you do this time, you stoopnagel?"

Percy didn't answer. He strode past the desk without saying a word, patting his hair with his fingers. He went through my office and into the storage shed. William Wharton answered for him. "Boss Dean? I think what he did was teach a certain french-fry it ain't smart to laugh at him," he said, and then began to laugh himself. It was a good laugh, a *country* laugh, cheery and deep. There were people I met during that period of my life (very scary people, for the most part) who only sounded normal when they laughed. Wild Bill Wharton was one of those.

I looked down at the mouse again, stunned. It was still breathing, but there were little minute beads of blood caught in the filaments of its whiskers, and a dull glaze was creeping over its previously brilliant oildrop eyes. Brutal picked up the colored spool, looked at it, then looked at me. He looked as dumbfounded as I felt. Behind us, Delacroix went on screaming out his grief and horror. It wasn't just the mouse, of course; Percy had smashed a hole in Delacroix's defenses and all his terror was pouring out. But Mr. Jingles was the focusing point for those pent-up feelings, and it was terrible to listen to him.

"Oh no," he cried over and over again, amid the screams and the garbled pleas and prayers in Cajun

French. "Oh no, oh no, poor Mr. Jingles, poor old Mr. Jingles, oh no."

"Give im to me."

I looked up, puzzled by that deep voice, at first not sure who it belonged to. I saw John Coffey. Like Delacroix, he had put his arms through the bars of his cell door, but unlike Del, he wasn't waving them around. He simply held them out as far as he could, the hands at the ends of them open. It was a purposeful pose, an almost urgent pose. And his voice had the same quality, which was why, I suppose, I didn't recognize it as belonging to Coffey at first. He seemed a different man from the lost, weepy soul that had occupied this cell for the last few weeks.

"Give im to me, Mr. Edgecombe! While there's still time!"

Then I remembered what he'd done for me, and understood. I supposed it couldn't hurt, but I didn't think it would do much good, either. When I picked the mouse up, I winced at the feel—there were so many splintered bones poking at various spots on Mr. Jingles's hide that it was like picking up a fur-covered pincushion. This was no urinary infection. Still—

"What are you doing?" Brutal asked as I put Mr. Jingles in Coffey's huge right hand. "What the hell?"

Coffey pulled the mouse back through the bars. He lay limp on Coffey's palm, tail hanging over the arc between Coffey's thumb and first finger, the tip twitching weakly in midair. Then Coffey covered his right hand with his left, creating a kind of cup in which the mouse lay. We could no longer see Mr.

Jingles himself, only the tail, hanging down and twitching at the tip like a dying pendulum. Coffey lifted his hands toward his face, spreading the fingers of the right as he did so, creating spaces like those between prison bars. The tail of the mouse now hung from the side of his hands that was facing us.

Brutal stepped next to me, still holding the colored spool between his fingers. "What's he think he's doing?"

"Shh," I said.

Delacroix had stopped screaming. "Please, John," he whispered. "Oh Johnny, help him, please help him, oh *s'il vous plaît.*"

Dean and Harry joined us, Harry with our old deck of Airplane cards still in one hand. "What's going on?" Dean asked, but I only shook my head. I was feeling hypnotized again, damned if I wasn't.

Coffey put his mouth between two of his fingers and inhaled sharply. For a moment everything hung suspended. Then he raised his head away from his hands and I saw the face of a man who looked desperately sick, or in terrible pain. His eyes were sharp and blazing; his upper teeth bit at his full lower lip; his dark face had faded to an unpleasant color that looked like ash stirred into mud. He made a choked sound way back in his throat.

"Dear Jesus Lord and Savior," Brutal whispered. His eyes appeared to be in danger of dropping right out of his face.

"What?" Harry almost barked. "*What?*"

"The tail! Don't you see it? The *tail!*"

4. DEATH OF EDUARD DELACROIX

Mr. Jingles's tail was no longer a dying pendulum; it was snapping briskly from side to side, like the tail of a cat in a bird-catching mood. And then, from inside Coffey's cupped hands, came a perfectly familiar squeak.

Coffey made that choking, gagging sound again, then turned his head to one side like a man that has coughed up a wad of phlegm and means to spit it out. Instead, he exhaled a cloud of black insects—I *think* they were insects, and the others said the same, but to this day I am not sure—from his mouth and nose. They boiled around him in a dark cloud that temporarily obscured his features.

"Christ, what're those?" Dean asked in a shrill, scared voice.

"It's all right," I heard myself say. "Don't panic, it's all right, in a few seconds they'll be gone."

As when Coffey had cured my urinary infection for me, the "bugs" turned white and then disappeared.

"Holy shit," Harry whispered.

"Paul?" Brutal asked in an unsteady voice. "Paul?"

Coffey looked okay again—like a fellow who has successfully coughed up a wad of meat that has been choking him. He bent down, put his cupped hands on the floor, peeked through his fingers, then opened them. Mr. Jingles, absolutely all right—not a single twist to his backbone, not a single lump poking at his hide—ran out. He paused for a moment at the door of Coffey's cell, then ran across the Green Mile to Delacroix's cell. As he went, I noticed there were still beads of blood in his whiskers.

Delacroix gathered him up, laughing and crying at the same time, covering the mouse with shameless, smacking kisses. Dean and Harry and Brutal watched with silent wonder. Then Brutal stepped forward and handed the colored spool through the bars. Delacroix didn't see it at first; he was too taken up with Mr. Jingles. He was like a father whose son has been saved from drowning. Brutal tapped him on the shoulder with the spool. Delacroix looked, saw it, took it, and went back to Mr. Jingles again, stroking his fur and devouring him with his eyes, needing to constantly refresh his perception that yes, the mouse was all right, the mouse was whole and fine and all right.

"Toss it," Brutal said. "I want to see how he runs."

"He all right, Boss Howell, he all right, praise God—"

"Toss it," Brutal repeated. "Mind me, Del."

Delacroix bent, clearly reluctant, clearly not wanting to let Mr. Jingles out of his hands again, at least not yet. Then, very gently, he tossed the spool. It rolled across the cell, past the Corona cigar box, and to the wall. Mr. Jingles was after it, but not quite with the speed he had shown previously. He appeared to be limping just a bit on his left rear leg, and that was what struck me the hardest—it was, I suppose, what made it real. That little limp.

He got to the spool, though, got to it just fine and nosed it back to Delacroix with all his old enthusiasm. I turned to John Coffey, who was standing at his cell door and smiling. It was a tired smile, and not what I'd call really happy, but the sharp urgency I'd seen in his face as he begged for the mouse to be given to him was gone, and so was the look of pain and fear, as if he were choking. It was our John Coffey again, with his not-quite-there face and strange, far-looking eyes.

"You helped it," I said. "Didn't you, big boy?"

"That's right," Coffey said. The smile widened a little, and for a moment or two it *was* happy. "I helped it. I helped Del's mouse. I helped ..." He trailed off, unable to remember the name.

"Mr. Jingles," Dean said. He was looking at John with careful, wondering eyes, as if he expected Coffey to burst into flames or maybe begin to float in his cell.

"That's right," Coffey said. "Mr. Jingles. He's a circus mouse. Goan live in ivy-glass."

"You bet your bobcat," Harry said, joining us in looking at John Coffey. Behind us, Delacroix lay down on his bunk with Mr. Jingles on his chest. Del was crooning to him, singing him some French song that sounded like a lullaby.

Coffey looked up the Green Mile toward the duty desk and the door which led into my office and the storage room beyond. "Boss Percy's bad," he said. "Boss Percy's mean. He stepped on Del's mouse. He stepped on Mr. Jingles."

And then, before we could say anything else to him—if we could have thought of anything to say—John Coffey went back to his bunk, lay down, and rolled on his side to face the wall.

3

Percy was standing with his back to us when Brutal and I came into the storage room about twenty minutes later. He had found a can of paste furniture polish on a shelf above the hamper where we put our dirty uniforms (and, sometimes, our civilian clothes; the prison laundry didn't care what it washed), and was polishing the oak arms and legs of the electric chair. This probably sounds bizarre to you, perhaps even macabre, but to Brutal and me, it seemed the most normal thing Percy had done all night. Old Sparky would be meeting his public tomorrow, and Percy would at least appear to be in charge.

"Percy," I said quietly.

He turned, the little tune he'd been humming dying in his throat, and looked at us. I didn't see the fear I'd expected, at least not at first. I realized that Percy looked older, somehow. And, I thought, John Coffey was right. He looked mean. Meanness is like an addicting drug—no one on earth is more qualified to say that than me—and I thought that, after a certain amount of experimentation, Percy had gotten hooked on it. He liked what he had done to Delacroix's mouse. What he liked even more was Delacroix's dismayed screams.

"Don't start in on me," he said in a tone of voice that was almost pleasant. "I mean, hey, it was just a mouse. It never belonged here in the first place, as you boys well know."

"The mouse is fine," I said. My heart was thumping hard in my chest but I made my voice come out mild, almost disinterested. "Just fine. Running and squeaking and chasing its spool again. You're no better at mouse-killing than you are at most of the other things you do around here."

He was looking at me, amazed and disbelieving. "You expect me to believe that? The goddam thing *crunched*! I heard it! So you can just—"

"Shut up."

He stared at me, his eyes wide. "*What*? What did you say to me?"

I took a step closer to him. I could feel a vein throbbing in the middle of my forehead. I couldn't remember the last time I'd felt so angry. "Aren't you glad Mr. Jingles is okay? After all the talks we've had about how our job is to keep the prisoners calm, especially when it gets near the end for them, I thought you'd be glad. Relieved. With Del having to take the walk tomorrow, and all."

Percy looked from me to Brutal, his studied calmness dissolving into uncertainty. "What the hell game do you boys think you're playing?" he asked.

"None of this is a game, my friend," Brutal said. "You thinking it is . . . well, that's just one of the reasons you can't be trusted. You want to know the absolute truth? I think you're a pretty sad case."

"You want to watch it," Percy said. Now there was a rawness in his voice. Fear creeping back in, after all—fear of what we might want with him, fear of what we might be up to. I was glad to hear it. It would make him easier to deal with. "I know people. Important people."

"So you say, but you're *such* a dreamer," Brutal said. He sounded as if he was on the verge of laughter.

Percy dropped the polishing rag onto the seat of the chair with the clamps attached to the arms and legs. "I killed that mouse," he said in a voice that was not quite steady.

"Go on and check for yourself," I said. "It's a free country."

"I will," he said. "I will."

He stalked past us, mouth set, small hands (Wharton was right, they *were* pretty) fiddling with his comb. He went up the steps and ducked through into my office. Brutal and I stood by Old Sparky, waiting for him to come back and not talking. I don't know about Brutal, but I couldn't think of a thing to say. I didn't even know how to think about what we had just seen.

Three minutes passed. Brutal picked up Percy's rag and began to polish the thick back-slats of the electric chair. He had time to finish one and start another before Percy came back. He stumbled and almost fell coming down the steps from the office to the storage-room floor, and when he crossed to us he came at an uneven strut. His face was shocked and unbelieving.

"You switched them," he said in a shrill, accusatory voice. "You switched mice somehow, you bastards. You're playing with me, and you're going to be goddam sorry if you don't stop! I'll see you on the goddam breadlines if you don't stop! Who do you think you are?"

He quit, panting for breath, his hands clenched.

"I'll tell you who we are," I said. "We're the people you work with, Percy . . . but not for very much longer." I reached out and clamped my hands on his shoulders. Not real hard; but it was a clamp, all right. Yes it was.

Percy reached up to break it. "Take your—"

Brutal grabbed his right hand—the whole thing, small and soft and white, disappeared into Brutal's tanned fist. "Shut up your cakehole, sonny. If you know what's good for you, you'll take this one last opportunity to dig the wax out of your ears."

I turned him around, lifted him onto the platform, then backed him up until the backs of his knees struck the seat of the electric chair and he had to sit down. His calm was gone; the meanness and the arrogance, too. Those things were real enough, but you have to remember that Percy was very young. At his age they were still only a thin veneer, like an ugly shade of enamel paint. You could still chip through. And I judged that Percy was now ready to listen.

"I want your word," I said.

"My word about what?" His mouth was still trying to sneer, but his eyes were terrified. The power in the switch room was locked off, but Old Sparky's wooden seat had its own power, and right then I judged that Percy was feeling it.

"Your word that if we put you out front for it tomorrow night, you'll really go on to Briar Ridge and leave us alone," Brutal said, speaking with a vehemence I had never heard from him before. "That you'll put in for a transfer the very next day."

"And if I won't? If I should just call up certain people and tell them you're harassing me and threatening me? *Bullying* me?"

"We might get the bum's rush if your connections are as good as you seem to think they are," I said, "but we'd make sure you left your fair share of blood on the floor, too, Percy."

"About that mouse? Huh! You think anyone is going to care that I stepped on a condemned murderer's pet mouse? Outside of this looneybin, that is?"

"No. But three men saw you just standing there with your thumb up your ass while Wild Bill Wharton was trying to strangle Dean Stanton with his wrist-chains. About that people *will* care, Percy, I promise you. About that even your offsides uncle the governor is going to care."

Percy's cheeks and brow flushed a patchy red. "You think they'd believe you?" he asked, but his voice had lost a lot of its angry force. Clearly *he* thought someone might believe us. And Percy didn't like being in trouble. Breaking the rules was okay. Getting caught breaking them was not.

"Well, I've got some photos of Dean's neck before the bruising went down," Brutal said—I had no idea if this was true or not, but it certainly sounded good. "You know what those pix say? That Wharton got a pretty good shot at it before anyone pulled him off, although you were right there, and on Wharton's blind side. You'd have some hard questions to answer, wouldn't you? And a thing like that could follow a man for quite a spell. Chances are it'd still be there long after his relatives were out of the state capital and back home drinking mint juleps on the front porch. A man's work-record can be a mighty interesting thing, and a lot of people get a chance to look at it over the course of a lifetime."

Percy's eyes flicked back and forth mistrustfully between us. His left hand went to his hair and smoothed it. He said nothing, but I thought we almost had him.

"Come on, let's quit this," I said. "You don't want to be here any more than we want you here, isn't that so?"

"I hate it here!" he burst out. "I hate the way you treat me, the way you never gave me a chance!"

That last was far from true, but I judged this wasn't the time to argue the matter.

"But I don't like to be pushed around, either. My Daddy taught me that once you start down that road you most likely end up letting people push you around your whole life." His eyes, not as pretty as his hands but almost, flashed. "I especially don't like being pushed around by big apes like this guy." He glanced at my old friend and grunted. "Brutal—you got the right nickname, at least."

"You have to understand something, Percy," I said. "The way we look at it, you've been pushing *us* around. We keep telling you the way we do things around here and you keep doing things your own way, then hiding behind your political connections when things turn out wrong. Stepping on Delacroix's mouse—" Brutal caught my eye and I backtracked in a hurry. "*Trying* to step on Delacroix's mouse is just a case in point. You push and push and push; we're finally pushing back, that's all. But listen, if you do right, you'll come out of this looking good—like a young man on his way up—and smelling like a rose. Nobody'll ever know about this little talk we're having. So what do you say? Act like a grownup. Promise you'll leave after Del."

He thought it over. And after a moment or two, a look came into his eyes, the sort of look a fellow gets when he's just had a good idea. I didn't like it much, because any idea which seemed good to Percy wouldn't seem good to us.

"If nothing else," Brutal said, "just think how nice it'd be to get away from that sack of pus Wharton."

Percy nodded, and I let him get out of the chair. He straightened his uniform shirt, tucked it in at the back, gave his hair a pass-through with his comb. Then he looked at us. "Okay, I agree. I'm out front for Del tomorrow night; I'll put in for Briar Ridge the very next day. We call it quits right there. Good enough?"

"Good enough," I said. That look was still in his eyes, but right then I was too relieved to care.

He stuck out his hand. "Shake on it?"

I did. So did Brutal.

More fools us.

4

The next day was the thickest yet, and the last of our strange October heat. Thunder was rumbling in the west when I came to work, and the dark clouds were beginning to stack up there. They moved closer as the night came down, and we could see blue-white forks of lightning jabbing out of them. There was a tornado in Trapingus County around ten that night—it killed four people and tore the roof off the livery stable in Tefton—and vicious thunderstorms and gale-force winds at Cold Mountain. Later it seemed to me as if the very heavens had protested the bad death of Eduard Delacroix.

Everything went just fine to begin with. Del had spent a quiet day in his cell, sometimes playing with Mr. Jingles but mostly just lying on his bunk and petting him. Wharton tried to get trouble started a couple of times—once he hollered down to Del about the mouseburgers they were going to have after old Lucky Pierre was dancing the two-step in hell—but the little Cajun didn't respond and Wharton, apparently deciding that was his best shot, gave it up.

At quarter past ten, Brother Schuster showed up and delighted us all by saying he would recite the Lord's Prayer with Del in Cajun French. It seemed like a good omen. In that we were wrong, of course.

The witnesses began to arrive around eleven, most talking in low tones about the impending weather, and speculating about the possibility of a power outage postponing the electrocution. None of them seemed to know that Old Sparky ran off a generator, and unless that took a direct lightning-hit, the show would go on. Harry was in the switch room that night, so he and Bill Dodge and Percy Wetmore acted as ushers, seeing folks into their seats and asking each one if he'd like a cold drink of water. There were two women present: the sister of the girl Del had raped and murdered, and the mother of one of the fire victims. The latter lady was large and pale and determined. She told Harry Terwilliger that she hoped the man she'd come to see was good and scared, that he knew the fires in the furnace were stoked for him, and that Satan's imps were waiting for him. Then she burst into tears and buried her face in a lace hanky that was almost the size of a pillow-slip.

Thunder, hardly muffled at all by the tin roof, banged harsh and loud. People glanced up uneasily. Men who looked uncomfortable wearing ties this late at night wiped at their florid cheeks. It was hotter than blue blazes in the storage shed. And, of course, they kept turning their eyes to Old Sparky. They might have made jokes about this chore earlier in the week, but the jokes were gone by eleven-thirty or so that night. I started all this by telling you that the humor went out of the situation in a hurry for the people who had to sit down in that oak chair, but the condemned prisoners weren't the only ones who lost the smiles off their faces when the time actually came. It just seemed so *bald*, somehow, squatting up there on its platform, with the clamps on the legs sticking off to either side, looking like the things a person with polio would have to wear. There wasn't much talk, and when the thunder boomed again, as sharp and personal as a splintering tree, the sister of Delacroix's victim gave a little scream. The last person to take his seat in the witness's section was Curtis Anderson, Warden Moores's stand-in.

At eleven-thirty, I approached Delacroix's cell with Brutal and Dean walking slightly behind me. Del was sitting on his bunk, with Mr. Jingles in his lap. The mouse's head was stretched forward toward the condemned man, his little oilspot eyes rapt on Del's face. Del was stroking the top of Mr. Jingles's head between his ears. Large silent tears were rolling down Del's face, and it was these the mouse seemed to be peering at. Del looked up at the sound of our footsteps. He was very pale. From behind me, I sensed rather than saw John Coffey standing at his cell door, watching.

Del winced at the sound of my keys clashing against metal, but held steady, continuing to stroke

Mr. Jingles's head, as I turned the locks and ran the door open.

"Hi dere, Boss Edgecombe," he said. "Hi dere, boys. Say hi, Mr. Jingles." But Mr. Jingles only continued to look raptly up at the balding little man's face, as if wondering at the source of his tears. The colored spool had been neatly laid aside in the Corona box— laid aside for the last time, I thought, and felt a pang.

"Eduard Delacroix, as an officer of the court ..."

"Boss Edgecombe?"

I thought about just running on with the set speech, then thought again. "What is it, Del?"

He held the mouse out to me. "Here. Don't let nothing happen to Mr. Jingles."

"Del, I don't think he'll come to me. He's not—"

"*Mais oui*, he say he will. He say he know all about you, Boss Edgecombe, and you gonna take him down to dat place in Florida where the mousies do their tricks. He say he trust you." He held his hand out farther, and I'll be damned if the mouse didn't step off his palm and onto my shoulder. It was so light I couldn't even feel it through my uniform coat, but I sensed it, like a small heat. "And boss? Don't let that bad 'un near him again. Don't let that bad 'un hurt my mouse."

"No, Del. I won't." The question was, what was I supposed to do with him right then? I couldn't very well march Delacroix past the witnesses with a mouse perched on my shoulder.

"I'll take him, boss," a voice rumbled from behind me. It was John Coffey's voice, and it was eerie the way it came right then, as though he had read my mind. "Just for now. If Del don't mind."

Del nodded, relieved. "Yeah, you take im, John, 'til dis foolishment done—*bien*! And den after . . ." His gaze shifted back to Brutal and me. "You gonna take him down to Florida. To dat Mouseville Place."

"Yeah, most likely Paul and I will do it together," Brutal said, watching with a troubled and unquiet eye as Mr. Jingles stepped off my shoulder and into Coffey's huge outstretched palm. Mr. Jingles did this with no protest or attempt to run; indeed, he scampered as readily up John Coffey's arm as he had stepped onto my shoulder. "We'll take some of our vacation time. Won't we, Paul?"

I nodded. Del nodded, too, eyes bright, just a trace of a smile on his lips. "People pay a dime apiece to see him. Two cents for the kiddies. Ain't dat right, Boss Howell?"

"That's right, Del."

"You a good man, Boss Howell," Del said. "You, too, Boss Edgecombe. You yell at me sometimes, *oui*, but not 'less you have to. You all good men except for dat Percy. I wish I coulda met you someplace else. *Mauvais temps, mauvaise chance.*"

"I got something to say to you, Del," I told him. "They're just the words I have to say to everyone before we walk. No big deal, but it's part of my job. Okay?"

"*Oui, monsieur*," he said, and looked at Mr. Jingles, perched on John Coffey's broad shoulder, for the last time. "*Au revoir, mon ami*," he said, beginning to cry harder. *"Je t'aime, mon petit."* He blew the mouse a kiss. It should have been funny, that blown kiss, or maybe just grotesque, but it wasn't. I met Dean's eye for a moment, then had to look away. Dean stared down the corridor toward the restraint room and smiled strangely. I believe he was on the verge of tears. As for me, I said what I had to say, beginning with the part about how I was an officer of the court, and when I was done, Delacroix stepped out of his cell for the last time.

"Hold on a second longer, hoss," Brutal said, and checked the crown of Del's head, where the cap would go. He nodded at me, then clapped Del on the shoulder. "Right with Eversharp. We're on our way."

So Eduard Delacroix took his last walk on the Green Mile with little streams of mingled sweat and tears running down his cheeks and big thunder rolling in the sky overhead. Brutal walked on the condemned man's left, I was on his right, Dean was to the rear.

Schuster was in my office, with guards Ringgold and Battle standing in the corners and keeping watch. Schuster looked up at Del, smiled, and then addressed him in French. It sounded stilted to me, but it worked wonders. Del smiled back, then went to Schuster, put his arms around him, hugged him. Ringgold and Battle tensed, but I raised my hands to them and shook my head.

Schuster listened to Del's flood of tear-choked French, nodded as if he understood perfectly, and patted him on the back. He looked at me over the little man's shoulder and said, "I hardly understand a quarter of what he's saying."

"Don't think it matters," Brutal rumbled.

"Neither do I, son," Schuster said with a grin. He was the best of them, and now I realize I have no idea what became of him. I hope he kept his faith, whatever else befell.

He urged Delacroix onto his knees, then folded his hands. Delacroix did the same.

"*Not' Père, qui êtes aux cieux*," Schuster began, and Delacroix joined him. They spoke the Lord's Prayer together in that liquid-sounding Cajun French, all the way to "*mais délivrez-nous du mal, ainsi soit-il.*" By then, Del's tears had mostly stopped and he looked calm. Some Bible verses (in English) followed, not neglecting the old standby about the still waters. When that was done, Schuster started to get up, but Del held onto the sleeve of his shirt and said something in French. Schuster listened carefully, frowning. He responded. Del said something else, then just looked at him hopefully.

Schuster turned to me and said: "He's got something else, Mr. Edgecombe. A prayer I can't help him with, because of my faith. Is it all right?"

I looked at the clock on the wall and saw it was seventeen minutes to midnight. "Yes," I said, "but it'll have to be quick. We've got a schedule to keep here, you know."

"Yes. I do." He turned to Delacroix and gave him a nod.

Del closed his eyes as if to pray, but for a moment

said nothing. A frown creased his forehead and I had a sense of him reaching far back in his mind, as a man may search a small attic room for an object which hasn't been used (or needed) for a long, long time. I glanced at the clock again and almost said something—would have, if Brutal hadn't twitched my sleeve and shaken his head.

Then Del began, speaking softly but quickly in that Cajun which was as round and soft and sensual as a young woman's breast: "*Marie! Je vous salue, Marie, oui, pleine de grâce; le Seigneur est avec vous; vous êtes bénie entre toutes les femmes, et mon cher Jésus, le fruit de vos entrailles, est béni.*" He was crying again, but I don't think he knew it. "*Sainte Marie, Ô ma mère, Mère de Dieu, priez pour moi, priez pour nous, pauv' pécheurs, maint'ant et à l'heure . . . l'heure de notre mort. L'heure de mon mort.*" He took a deep, shuddering breath. "*Ainsi soit-il.*"

Lightning spilled through the room's one window in a brief blue-white glare as Delacroix got to his feet. Everyone jumped and cringed except for Del himself; he still seemed lost in the old prayer. He reached out with one hand, not looking to see where it went. Brutal took it and squeezed it briefly. Delacroix looked at him and smiled a little. "*Nous voyons—*" he began, then stopped. With a conscious effort, he switched back to English. "We can go now, Boss Howell, Boss Edgecombe. I'm right wit God."

"That's good," I said, wondering how right with God Del was going to feel twenty minutes from now, when he stood on the other side of the electricity. I hoped his last prayer had been heard, and that Mother Mary was praying for him with all her heart and soul, because Eduard Delacroix, rapist and murderer, right then needed all the praying he could get his hands on. Outside, thunder bashed across the sky again. "Come on, Del. Not far now."

"Fine, boss, dat fine. Because I ain't ascairt no more." So he said, but I saw in his eyes that—Our Father or no Our Father, Hail Mary or no Hail Mary—he lied. By the time they cross the rest of the green carpet and duck through the little door, almost all of them are scared.

"Stop at the bottom, Del," I told him in a low voice as he went through, but it was advice I needn't have given him. He stopped at the foot of the stairs, all right, stopped cold, and what did it was the sight of Percy Wetmore standing there on the platform, with the sponge-bucket by one foot and the phone that went to the governor just visible beyond his right hip.

"*Non*," Del said in a low, horrified voice. "*Non, non*, not him!"

"Walk on," Brutal said. "You just keep your eyes on me and Paul. Forget he's there at all."

"But—"

People had turned to look at us, but by moving my body a bit, I could still grip Delacroix's left elbow without being seen. "Steady," I said in a voice only Del—and perhaps Brutal—could hear. "The only thing most of these people will remember about you is how you go out, so give them something good."

The loudest crack of thunder yet broke overhead at that moment, loud enough to make the storage room's tin roof vibrate. Percy jumped as if someone had goosed him, and Del gave a small, contemptuous snort of laughter. "It get much louder dan dat, he gonna piddle in his pants again," he said, and then squared his shoulders—not that he had much to square. "Come on. Let's get it over."

We walked to the platform. Delacroix ran a nervous eye over the witnesses—about twenty-five of them this time—as we went, but Brutal, Dean, and I kept our own eyes trained on the chair. All looked in order to me. I raised one thumb and a questioning eyebrow to Percy, who gave a little one-sided grimace, as if to say *What do you mean, is everything all right? Of course it is.*

I hoped he was right.

Brutal and I reached automatically for Delacroix's elbows as he stepped up onto the platform. It's only eight or so inches up from the floor, but you'd be surprised how many of them, even the toughest of tough babies, need help to make that last step up of their lives.

Del did okay, though. He stood in front of the chair for a moment (resolutely not looking at Percy), then actually spoke to it, as if introducing himself: *"C'est moi,"* he said. Percy reached for him, but Delacroix turned around on his own and sat down. I knelt on what was now his left side, and Brutal knelt on his right. I guarded my crotch and my throat in the manner I have already described, then swung the clamp in so that its open jaws encircled the skinny white flesh just above the Cajun's ankle. Thunder bellowed and I jumped. Sweat ran in my eye, stinging. Mouseville, I kept thinking for some reason. Mouseville, and how it cost a dime to get in. Two cents for the kiddies, who would look at Mr. Jingles through his ivy-glass windows.

The clamp was balky, wouldn't shut. I could hear Del breathing in great dry pulls of air, lungs that would be charred bags less than four minutes from now laboring to keep up with his fear-driven heart. The fact that he had killed half a dozen people seemed at that moment the least important thing about him. I'm not trying to say anything about right and wrong here, but only to tell how it was.

Dean knelt next to me and whispered, "What's wrong, Paul?"

"I can't—" I began, and then the clamp closed with an audible snapping sound. It must have also pinched a fold of Delacroix's skin in its jaws, because he flinched and made a little hissing noise. "Sorry," I said.

"It okay, boss," Del said. "It only gonna hurt for a minute."

Brutal's side had the clamp with the electrode in it, which always took a little longer, and so we stood up, all three of us, at almost exactly the same time. Dean reached for the wrist-clamp on Del's left, and Percy went to the one on his right. I was ready to move forward if Percy should need help, but he did better with his wrist-clamp than I'd done with my ankle-clamp. I could see Del trembling all over now, as if a low current were already passing through him. I could smell his sweat, too. It was sour and strong and reminded me of weak pickle juice.

Dean nodded to Percy. Percy turned back over his shoulder—I could see a place just under the angle of his jaw where he'd cut himself shaving that day—and said in a low, firm voice: "Roll on one!"

There was a hum, sort of like the sound an old refrigerator makes when it kicks on, and the hanging lights in the storage room brightened. There were a few low gasps and murmurs from the audience. Del jerked in the chair, his hands gripping the ends of the oak arms hard enough to turn the knuckles white. His eyes rolled rapidly from side to side in their sockets, and his dry breathing quickened even more. He was almost panting now.

"Steady," Brutal murmured. "Steady, Del, you're doing just fine. Hang on, you're doing just fine."

Hey you guys! I thought. *Come and see what Mr. Jingles can do!* And overhead, the thunder banged again.

Percy stepped grandly around to the front of the electric chair. This was his big moment, he was at center stage, all eyes were on him. All, that was, but for one set. Delacroix saw who it was and looked down at his lap instead. I would have bet you a dollar to a doughnut that Percy would flub his lines when he actually had to say them for an audience, but he reeled them off without a hitch, in an eerily calm voice.

"Eduard Delacroix, you have been condemned to die in the electric chair, sentence passed by a jury of your peers and imposed by a judge of good standing in this state, God save the people of this state. Do you have anything to say before sentence is carried out?"

Del tried to speak and at first nothing came out but a terrified whisper full of air and vowel-sounds. The shadow of a contemptuous smile touched the corners of Percy's lips, and I could have cheerfully shot him right there. Then Del licked his lips and tried again.

"I sorry for what I do," he said. "I give anything to turn back the clock, but no one can. So now—" Thunder exploded like an airburst mortar shell above us. Del jumped as much as the clamps would allow, eyes starting wildly out of his wet face. "So now I pay the price. God forgive me." He licked his lips again, and looked at Brutal. "Don't forget your promise about Mr. Jingles," he said in a lower voice that was meant just for us.

"We won't, don't worry," I said, and patted Delacroix's clay-cold hand. "He's going to Mouseville—"

"The hell he is," Percy said, speaking from the corner of his mouth like a yardwise con as he hooked the restraining belt across Delacroix's chest. "There's no such place. It's a fairy-tale these guys made up to keep you quiet. Just thought you should know, faggot."

A stricken light in Del's eyes told me that part of him *had* known ... but would have kept the knowledge from the rest of him, if allowed. I looked at

Percy, dumbfounded and furious, and he looked back at me levelly, as if to ask what I meant to do about it. And he had me, of course. There was nothing I *could* do about it, not in front of the witnesses, not with Delacroix now sitting on the furthest edge of life. There was nothing to do now but go on with it, finish it.

Percy took the mask from its hook and rolled it down over Del's face, snugging it tight under the little man's undershot chin so as to stretch the hole in the top. Taking the sponge from the bucket and putting it in the cap was the next, and it was here that Percy diverged from the routine for the first time: instead of just bending over and fishing the sponge out, he took the steel cap from the back of the chair, and bent over with it in his hands. Instead of bringing the sponge to the cap, in other words—which would have been the natural way to do it—he brought the cap to the sponge. I should have realized something was wrong, but I was too upset. It was the only execution I ever took part in where I felt totally out of control. As for Brutal, he never looked at Percy at all, not as Percy bent over the bucket (moving so as to partially block what he was doing from our view), not as he straightened up and turned to Del with the cap in his hands and the brown circle of sponge already inside it. Brutal was looking at the cloth which had replaced Del's face, watching the way the black silk mask drew in, outlining the circle of Del's open mouth, and then puffed out again with his breath. There were big beads of perspiration on

Brutal's forehead, and at his temples, just below the hairline. I had never seen him sweat at an execution before. Behind him, Dean looked distracted and ill, as if he was fighting not to lose his supper. We all understood that something was wrong, I know that now. We just couldn't tell what it was. No one knew—not then—about the questions Percy had been asking Jack Van Hay. There were a lot of them, but I suspect most were just camouflage. What Percy wanted to know about—the *only* thing Percy wanted to know about, I believe—was the sponge. The purpose of the sponge. Why it was soaked in brine . . . and what would happen if it was not soaked in brine.

What would happen if the sponge was dry.

Percy jammed the cap down on Del's head. The little man jumped and moaned again, this time louder. Some of the witnesses stirred uneasily on their folding chairs. Dean took a half-step forward, meaning to help with the chin-strap, and Percy motioned him curtly to step back. Dean did, hunching a little and wincing as another blast of thunder shook the storage shed. This time it was followed by the first spatters of rain across the roof. They sounded hard, like someone flinging handfuls of goobers onto a washboard.

You've heard people say "My blood ran cold" about things, haven't you? Sure. All of us have, but the only time in all my years that I actually felt it happen to me was on that new and thunderstruck morning in October of 1932, at about ten seconds past midnight. It wasn't the look of poison triumph on Percy Wetmore's face as he stepped away from the capped, clamped, and hooded figure sitting there in Old Sparky; it was what I should have seen and didn't. There was no water running down Del's cheeks from out of the cap. That was when I finally got it.

"Edward Delacroix," Percy was saying, "electricity shall now be passed through your body until you are dead, according to state law."

I looked over at Brutal in an agony that made my urinary infection seem like a bumped finger. *The sponge is dry!* I mouthed at him, but he only shook his head, not understanding, and looked back at the mask over the Frenchman's face, where the man's last few breaths were pulling the black silk in and then blousing it out again.

I reached for Percy's elbow and he stepped away from me, giving me a flat look as he did so. It was only a momentary glance, but it told me everything. Later he would tell his lies and his half-truths, and most would be believed by the people who mattered, but I knew a different story. Percy was a good student when he was doing something he cared about, we'd found that out at the rehearsals, and he had listened carefully when Jack Van Hay explained how the brine-soaked sponge conducted the juice, channelling it, turning the charge into a kind of electric bullet to the brain. Oh yes, Percy knew exactly what he was doing. I think I believed him later when he said he didn't know how far it would go, but that doesn't even count in the good-intentions column, does it? I don't think so. Yet, short of screaming in front of the assistant warden and all the witnesses for Jack Van Hay not to pull the switch, there was nothing I could do. Given another five seconds, I think I might have screamed just that, but Percy didn't give me another five seconds.

"May God have mercy on your soul," he told the panting, terrified figure in the electric chair, then looked past him at the mesh-covered rectangle where Harry and Jack were standing, Jack with his hand on the switch marked MABEL'S HAIR DRIER. The doctor was standing to the right of that window, eyes fixed on the black bag between his feet, as silent and self-effacing as ever. "Roll on two!"

At first it was the same as always—the humming that was a little louder than the original cycle-up, but not much, and the mindless forward surge of Del's body as his muscles spasmed.

Then things started going wrong.

The humming lost its steadiness and began to waver. It was joined by a crackling sound, like cellophane being crinkled. I could smell something horrible that I didn't identify as a mixture of burning hair and organic sponge until I saw blue tendrils of smoke curling out from beneath the edges of the cap. More smoke was streaming out of the hole in the top of the cap that the wire came in through; it looked like smoke coming out of the hole in an Indian's teepee.

Delacroix began to jitter and twist in the chair, his

mask-covered face snapping from side to side as if in some vehement refusal. His legs began to piston up and down in short strokes that were hampered by the clamps on his ankles. Thunder banged overhead, and now the rain began to pour down harder.

I looked at Dean Stanton; he stared wildly back. There was a muffled pop from under the cap, like a pine knot exploding in a hot fire, and now I could see smoke coming through the mask, as well, seeping out in little curls.

I lunged toward the mesh between us and the switch room, but before I could open my mouth, Brutus Howell seized my elbow. His grip was hard enough to make the nerves in there tingle. He was as white as tallow but not in a panic—not even close to being in a panic. "Don't you tell Jack to stop," he said in a low voice. "Whatever you do, don't tell him that. It's too late to stop."

At first, when Del began to scream, the witnesses didn't hear him. The rain on the tin roof had swelled to a roar, and the thunder was damned near continuous. But those of us on the platform heard him, all right—choked howls of pain from beneath the smoking mask, sounds an animal caught and mangled in a hay-baler might make.

The hum from the cap was ragged and wild now, broken by bursts of what sounded like radio static. Delacroix began to slam back and forth in the chair like a kid doing a tantrum. The platform shook, and he hit the leather restraining belt almost hard enough to pop it. The current was also twisting him from side to side, and I heard the crunching snap as his right shoulder either broke or dislocated. It went with a sound like someone hitting a wooden crate with a sledgehammer. The crotch of his pants, no more than a blur because of the short pistoning strokes of his legs, darkened. Then he began to squeal, horrible sounds, high-pitched and ratlike, that were audible even over the rushing downpour.

"What the hell's happening to him?" someone cried.

"Are those clamps going to hold?"

"Christ, the *smell*! Phew!"

Then, one of the two women: "Is this normal?"

Delacroix snapped forward, dropped back, snapped forward, fell back. Percy was staring at him with slack-jawed horror. He had expected *something*, sure, but not this.

The mask burst into flame on Delacroix's face. The smell of cooking hair and sponge was now joined by the smell of cooking flesh. Brutal grabbed the bucket the sponge had been in—it was empty now, of course—and charged for the extra-deep janitor's sink in the corner.

"Shouldn't I kill the juice, Paul?" Van Hay called through the mesh. He sounded completely rattled. "Shouldn't I—"

"No!" I shouted back. Brutal had understood it first, but I hadn't been far behind: we had to finish it. Whatever else we might do in all the rest of our lives was secondary to that one thing: we had to finish with Delacroix. "Roll, for Christ's sake! Roll, roll, roll!"

I turned to Brutal, hardly aware of the people talking behind us now, some on their feet, a couple screaming. "*Quit that!*" I yelled at Brutal. "*No water! No water! Are you nuts?*"

Brutal turned toward me, a kind of dazed understanding on his face. Throw water on a man who was getting the juice. Oh yes. That would be very smart. He looked around, saw the chemical fire extinguisher hanging on the wall, and got that instead. Good boy.

The mask had peeled away from Delacroix's face enough to reveal features that had gone blacker than John Coffey's. His eyes, now nothing but misshapen globs of white, filmy jelly, had been blown out of their sockets and lay on his cheeks. His eyelashes were gone, and as I looked, the lids themselves caught fire and began to burn. Smoke puffed from the open V of his shirt. And still the humming of the electricity went on and on, filling my head, vibrating in there. I think it's the sound mad people must hear, that or something like it.

Dean started forward, thinking in some dazed way that he could beat the fire out of Del's shirt with his hands, and I yanked him away almost hard enough to pull him off his feet. Touching Delacroix at that point would have been like Brer Rabbit punching into the Tar-Baby. An electrified Tar-Baby, in this case.

I still didn't turn around to see what was going on

behind us, but it sounded like pandemonium, chairs falling over, people bellowing, a woman crying *"Stop it, stop it, oh can't you see he's had enough?"* at the top of her lungs. Curtis Anderson grabbed my shoulder and asked what was happening, for Christ's sake, what was happening, and why didn't I order Jack to shut down?

"Because I can't," I said. "We've gone too far to turn back, can't you see that? It'll be over in a few more seconds, anyway."

But it was at least two minutes before it was over, the longest two minutes of my whole life, and through most of it I think Delacroix was conscious. He screamed and jittered and rocked from side to side. Smoke poured from his nostrils and from a mouth that had gone the purple-black of ripe plums. Smoke drifted up from his tongue the way smoke rises from a hot griddle. All the buttons on his shirt either burst or melted. His undershirt did not quite catch fire, but it charred and smoke poured through it and we could smell his chest-hair roasting. Behind us, people were heading for the door like cattle in a stampede. They couldn't get out through it, of course—we were in a damn prison, after all—so they simply clustered around it while Delacroix fried (*Now I'm fryin,* Old Toot had said when we were rehearsing for Arlen Bitterbuck, *I'm a done tom turkey*) and the thunder rolled and the rain ran down out of the sky in a perfect fury.

At some point I thought of the doc and looked

around for him. He was still there, but crumpled on the floor beside his black bag. He'd fainted.

Brutal came up and stood beside me, holding the fire extinguisher.

"Not yet," I said.

"I know."

We looked around for Percy and saw him standing almost behind Sparky now, frozen, eyes huge, one knuckle crammed into his mouth.

Then, at last, Delacroix slumped back in the chair, his bulging, misshapen face lying over on one shoulder. He was still jittering, but we'd seen this before; it was the current running through him. The cap had come askew on his head, but when we took it off a little later, most of his scalp and his remaining fringe of hair came with it, bonded to the metal as if by some powerful adhesive.

"Kill it!" I called to Jack when thirty seconds had gone by with nothing but electric jitters coming from the smoking, man-shaped lump of charcoal lolling in the electric chair. The hum died immediately, and I nodded to Brutal.

He turned and slammed the fire extinguisher into Percy's arms so hard that Percy staggered backward and almost fell off the platform. "You do it," Brutal said. "You're running the show, after all, ain't you?"

Percy gave him a look that was both sick and murderous, then armed the extinguisher, pumped it, cocked it, and shot a huge cloud of white foam over the man in the chair. I saw Del's foot twitch once as the spray hit his face and thought *Oh no, we might have to go again*, but there was only that single twitch.

Anderson had turned around and was bawling at the panicky witnesses, telling them everything was all right, everything was under control, just a power-surge from the electrical storm, nothing to worry about. Next thing, he'd be telling them that what they smelled—a devil's mixture of burned hair, fried meat, and fresh-baked shit—was Chanel No. 5.

"Get doc's stethoscope," I told Dean as the extinguisher ran dry. Delacroix was coated with white now, and the worst of the stench was being overlaid by a thin and bitter chemical smell.

"Doc ... should I ..."

"Never mind doc, just get his stethoscope," I said. "Let's get this over ... get him out of here."

Dean nodded. *Over* and *out of here* were two concepts that appealed to him just then. They appealed to both of us. He went over to doc's bag and began rummaging in it. Doc was beginning to move again, so at least he hadn't had a stroke or a heart-storm. That was good. But the way Brutal was looking at Percy wasn't.

"Get down in the tunnel and wait by the gurney," I said.

Percy swallowed. "Paul, listen. I didn't know—"

"Shut up. Get down in the tunnel and wait by the gurney. Now."

He swallowed, grimaced as if it hurt, and then walked toward the door which led to the stairs and the tunnel. He carried the empty fire extinguisher in his arms, as if it were a baby. Dean passed him, coming back to me with the stethoscope. I snatched it and set the earpieces. I'd done this before, in the army, and it's sort of like riding a bike—you don't forget.

I wiped at the foam on Delacroix's chest, then had to gag back vomit as a large, hot section of his skin simply slid away from the flesh beneath, the way the skin will slide off a . . . well, you know. A done tom turkey.

"Oh my God!" a voice I didn't recognize almost sobbed behind me. "Is it always this way? Why didn't somebody tell me? I never would have come!"

Too late now, friend, I thought. "Get that man out of here," I said to Dean or Brutal or whoever might be listening—I said it when I was sure I could speak without puking into Delacroix's smoking lap. "Get them all back by the door."

I steeled myself as best I could, then put the disc of the stethoscope on the red-black patch of raw flesh I'd made on Del's chest. I listened, praying I would hear nothing, and that's just what I did hear.

"He's dead," I told Brutal.

"Thank Christ."

"Yes. Thank Christ. You and Dean get the stretcher. Let's unbuckle him and get him out of here, fast."

5

We got his body down the twelve stairs and onto the gurney all right. My nightmare was that his cooked flesh might slough right off his bones as we lugged him—it was Old Toot's done tom turkey that had gotten into my head—but of course that didn't happen.

Curtis Anderson was upstairs soothing the spectators—trying to, anyway—and that was good for Brutal, because Anderson wasn't there to see when Brutal took a step toward the head of the gurney and pulled his arm back to slug Percy, who was standing there looking stunned. I caught his arm, and that was good for both of them. It was good for Percy because Brutal meant to deliver a blow of near-decapitory force, and good for Brutal because he would have lost his job if the blow had connected, and maybe ended up in prison himself.

"No," I said.

"What do you mean, no?" he asked me furiously. "How can you say no? You saw what he did! What are you telling me? That you're still going to let his *connections* protect him? After what he *did*?"

"Yes."

Brutal stared at me, mouth agape, eyes so angry they were watering.

"Listen to me, Brutus—you take a poke at him, and most likely we all go. You, me, Dean, Harry, maybe even Jack Van Hay. Everyone else moves a rung or two up the ladder, starting with Bill Dodge, and the Prison Commission hires three or four Breadline Barneys to fill the spots at the bottom. Maybe you can live with that, but—" I cocked my thumb at Dean, who was staring down the dripping, brick-lined tunnel. He was holding his specs in one hand, and looked almost as dazed as Percy. "But what about Dean? He's got two kids, one in high school and one just about to go."

"So what's it come down to?" Brutal asked. "We let him get away with it?"

"I didn't know the sponge was supposed to be wet," Percy said in a faint, mechanical voice. This was the story he had rehearsed beforehand, of course, when he was expecting a painful prank instead of the cataclysm we had just witnessed. "It was never wet when we rehearsed."

"Aw, you sucker—" Brutal began, and started for Percy. I grabbed him again and yanked him back. Footsteps clacked on the steps. I looked up, desperately afraid of seeing Curtis Anderson, but it was Harry Terwilliger. His cheeks were paper-white and his lips were purplish, as if he'd been eating black-berry cobbler.

I switched my attention back to Brutal. "For God's sake, Brutal, Delacroix's *dead*, nothing can change that, and Percy's not worth it." Was the plan, or the beginnings of it, in my head even then? I've won-dered about that since, let me tell you. I've wondered over the course of a lot of years, and have never been able to come up with a satisfactory answer. I suppose it doesn't matter much. A lot of things don't matter, but it doesn't keep a man from wondering about them, I've noticed.

"You guys talk about me like I was a chump," Percy said. He still sounded dazed and winded—as if someone had punched him deep in the gut—but he was coming back a little.

"You *are* a chump, Percy," I said.

"Hey, you can't—"

I controlled my own urge to hit him only with the greatest effort. Water dripped hollowly from the bricks down in the tunnel; our shadows danced huge and misshapen on the walls, like shadows in that Poe story about the big ape in the Rue Morgue. Thunder bashed, but down here it was muffled.

"I only want to hear one thing from you, Percy, and that's you repeating your promise to put in for Briar Ridge tomorrow."

"Don't worry about that," he said sullenly. He looked at the sheeted figure on the gurney, looked away, flicked his eyes up toward my face for a mo-ment, then looked away again.

"That *would* be for the best," Harry said. "Otherwise, you might get to know Wild Bill Wharton a whole lot better than you want to." A slight pause. "We could see to it."

Percy was afraid of us, and he was probably afraid of what we might do if he was still around when we found out he'd been talking to Jack Van Hay about what the sponge was for and why we always soaked it in brine, but Harry's mention of Wharton woke real terror in his eyes. I could see him remembering how Wharton had held him, ruffling his hair and crooning to him.

"You wouldn't dare," Percy whispered.

"Yes I would," Harry replied calmly. "And do you know what? I'd get away with it. Because you've already shown yourself to be careless as hell around the prisoners. Incompetent, too."

Percy's fists bunched and his cheeks colored in a thin pink. "I am not—"

"Sure you are," Dean said, joining us. We formed a rough semicircle around Percy at the foot of the stairs, and even a retreat up the tunnel was blocked; the gurney was behind him, with its load of smoking flesh hidden under an old sheet. "You just burned Delacroix alive. If that ain't incompetent, what is?"

Percy's eyes flickered. He had been planning to cover himself by pleading ignorance, and now he saw he was hoist by his own petard. I don't know what he might have said next, because Curtis Anderson came lunging down the stairs just then.

We heard him and drew back from Percy a little, so as not to look quite so threatening.

"What in the blue fuck was *that* all about?" Anderson roared. "Jesus Christ, there's puke all over the floor up there! And the smell! I got Magnusson and Old Toot-Toot to open both doors, but that smell won't come out for five damn years, that's what I'm betting. And that asshole Wharton is *singing* about it! I can hear him!"

"Can he carry a tune, Curt?" Brutal asked. You know how you can burn off illuminating gas with a single spark and not be hurt if you do it before the concentration gets too heavy? This was like that. We took an instant to gape at Brutus, and then we were all howling. Our high, hysterical laughter flapped up and down the gloomy tunnel like bats. Our shadows bobbed and flickered on the walls. Near the end, even Percy joined in. At last it died, and in its aftermath we all felt a little better. Felt *sane* again.

"Okay, boys," Anderson said, mopping at his teary eyes with his handkerchief and still snorting out an occasional hiccup of laughter, "what the hell happened?"

"An execution," Brutal said. I think his even tone surprised Anderson, but it didn't surprise me, at least not much; Brutal had always been good at turning down his dials in a hurry. "A successful one."

"How in the name of Christ can you call a direct-current abortion like that a success? We've got witnesses that won't sleep for a month! Hell, that fat old broad probably won't sleep for a year!"

Brutal pointed at the gurney, and the shape under the sheet. "He's dead, ain't he? As for your witnesses, most of them will be telling their friends tomorrow night that it was poetic justice—Del there burned a bunch of people alive, so we turned around and burned *him* alive. Except they won't say it was us. They'll say it was the will of God, working *through* us. Maybe there's even some truth to that. And you want to know the best part? The absolute cat's pajamas? Most of their friends will wish they'd been here to see it." He gave Percy a look both distasteful and sardonic as he said this last.

"And if their feathers are a little ruffled, so what?" Harry asked. "They volunteered for the damn job, nobody drafted them."

"I didn't know the sponge was supposed to be wet," Percy said in his robot's voice. "It's never wet in rehearsal."

Dean looked at him with utter disgust. "How many years did you spend pissing on the toilet seat before someone told you to put it up before you start?" he snarled.

Percy opened his mouth to reply, but I told him to shut up. For a wonder, he did. I turned to Anderson.

"Percy fucked up, Curtis—that's what happened, pure and simple." I turned toward Percy, daring him to contradict me. He didn't, maybe because he read my eyes: better that Anderson hear *stupid mistake* than *on purpose*. And besides, whatever was said down here in the tunnel didn't matter. What mattered, what always matters to the Percy Wetmores of the world, is what gets written down or overheard by the big bugs—the people who matter. What matters to the Percys of the world is how it plays in the newspapers.

Anderson looked at the five of us uncertainly. He even looked at Del, but Del wasn't talking. "I guess it could be worse," Anderson said.

"That's right," I agreed. "He could still be alive."

Curtis blinked—that possibility seemed not to have crossed his mind. "I want a complete report about this on my desk tomorrow," he said. "And none of you are going to talk to Warden Moores about it until I've had my chance. Are you?"

We shook our heads vehemently. If Curtis Anderson wanted to tell the warden, why, that was fine by us.

"If none of those asshole scribblers put it in their papers—"

"They won't," I said. "If they tried, their editors'd kill it. Too gruesome for a family audience. But they won't even try—they were all vets tonight. Sometimes things go wrong, that's all. They know it as well as we do."

Anderson considered a moment longer, then nodded. He turned his attention to Percy, an expression of disgust on his usually pleasant face. "You're a little asshole," he said, "and I don't like you a bit." He nodded at Percy's look of flabbergasted surprise. "If you tell any of your candy-ass friends I said that, I'll deny it until Aunt Rhody's old gray goose comes back to life, and these men will back me up. You've got a problem, son."

He turned and started up the stairs. I let him get four steps and then said: "Curtis?"

He turned back, eyebrows raised, saying nothing.

"You don't want to worry too much about Percy," I said. "He's moving on to Briar Ridge soon. Bigger and better things. Isn't that right, Percy?"

"As soon as his transfer comes through," Brutal added.

"And until it comes, he's going to call in sick every night," Dean put in.

That roused Percy, who hadn't been working at the prison long enough to have accumulated any paid sick-time. He looked at Dean with bright distaste. "Don't you *wish*," he said.

6

We were back on the block by one-fifteen or so (except for Percy, who had been ordered to clean up the storage room and was sulking his way through the job), me with a report to write. I decided to do it at the duty desk; if I sat in my more comfortable office chair, I'd likely doze off. That probably sounds peculiar to you, given what had happened only an hour before, but I felt as if I'd lived three lifetimes since eleven o'clock the previous night, all of them without sleep.

John Coffey was standing at his cell door, tears streaming from his strange, distant eyes—it was like watching blood run out of some unhealable but strangely painless wound. Closer to the desk, Wharton was sitting on his bunk, rocking from side to side, and singing a song apparently of his own invention, and not quite nonsense. As well as I can remember, it went something like this:

"Bar-be-cue! Me and you!
Stinky, pinky, phew-phew-phew!

It wasn't Billy or Philadelphia Philly,
it wasn't Jackie or Roy!
It was a warm little number, a hot cucumber,
by the name of Delacroix!"

"Shut up, you jerk," I said.

Wharton grinned, showing his mouthful of dingy teeth. *He* wasn't dying, at least not yet; he was up, happy, practically tap-dancing. "Come on in here and make me, why don't you?" he said happily, and then began another verse of "The Barbecue Song," making up words not quite at random. There was something going on in there, all right. A kind of green and stinking intelligence that was, in its own way, almost brilliant.

I went down to John Coffey. He wiped away his tears with the heels of his hands. His eyes were red and sore-looking, and it came to me that he was exhausted, too. Why he should have been, a man who trudged around the exercise yard maybe two hours a day and either sat or laid down in his cell the rest of the time, I didn't know, but I didn't doubt what I was seeing. It was too clear.

"Poor Del," he said in a low, hoarse voice. "Poor old Del."

"Yes," I said. "Poor old Del. John, are *you* okay?"

"He's out of it," Coffey said. "Del's out of it. Isn't he, boss?"

"Yes. Answer my question, John. Are you okay?"

"Del's out of it, he's the lucky one. No matter how it happened, he's the lucky one."

I thought Delacroix might have given him an argument on that, but didn't say so. I glanced around Coffey's cell, instead. "Where's Mr. Jingles?"

"Ran down there." He pointed through the bars, down the hall to the restraint-room door.

I nodded. "Well, he'll be back."

But he wasn't; Mr. Jingles's days on the Green Mile were over. The only trace of him we ever happened on was what Brutal found that winter: a few brightly colored splinters of wood, and a smell of peppermint candy wafting out of a hole in a beam.

I meant to walk away then, but I didn't. I looked at John Coffey, and he back at me as if he knew everything I was thinking. I told myself to get moving, to just call it a night and get moving, back to the duty desk and my report. Instead I said his name: "John Coffey."

"Yes, boss," he said at once.

Sometimes a man is cursed with needing to know a thing, and that was how it was with me right then. I dropped down on one knee and began taking off one of my shoes.

7

The rain had quit by the time I got home, and a late grin of moon had appeared over the ridges to the north. My sleepiness seemed to have gone with the clouds. I was wide awake, and I could smell Delacroix on me. I thought I might smell him on my skin—barbecue, me and you, stinky, pinky, phew-phew-phew—for a long time to come.

Janice was waiting up, as she always did on execution nights. I meant not to tell her the story, saw no sense in harrowing her with it, but she got a clear look at my face as I came in the kitchen door and would have it all. So I sat down, took her warm hands in my cold ones (the heater in my old Ford barely worked, and the weather had turned a hundred and eighty degrees since the storm), and told her what she thought she wanted to hear. About halfway through I broke down crying, which I hadn't expected. I was a little ashamed, but only a little; it was her, you see, and she never taxed me with the times that I slipped from the way I thought a man should be ... the way I thought *I* should be, at any rate. A

man with a good wife is the luckiest of God's crea-
tures, and one without must be among the most mis-
erable, I think, the only true blessing of their lives
that they don't know how poorly off they are. I cried,
and she held my head against her breast, and when
my own storm passed, I felt better ... a little, anyway. And I believe that was when I had the first conscious sight of my idea. Not the shoe; I don't mean
that. The shoe was related, but different. All my *real*
idea was right then, however, was an odd realization:
that John Coffey and Melinda Moores, different as
they might have been in size and sex and skin color,
had exactly the same eyes: woeful, sad, and distant.
Dying eyes.

"Come to bed," my wife said at last. "Come to bed
with me, Paul."

So I did, and we made love, and when it was over
she went to sleep. As I lay there watching the moon
grin and listening to the walls tick—they were at last
pulling in, exchanging summer for fall—I thought
about John Coffey saying he had helped it. *I helped
Del's mouse. I helped Mr. Jingles. He's a circus mouse.*
Sure. And maybe, I thought, we were all circus mice,
running around with only the dimmest awareness
that God and all His heavenly host were watching us
in our Bakelite houses through our ivy-glass windows.

I slept a little as the day began to lighten—two
hours, I guess, maybe three; and I slept the way I always sleep these days here in Georgia Pines and
hardly ever did then, in thin little licks. What I went

to sleep thinking about was the churches of my youth. The names changed, depending on the whims of my mother and her sisters, but they were all really the same, all The First Backwoods Church of Praise Jesus, The Lord Is Mighty. In the shadow of those blunt, square steeples, the concept of atonement came up as regularly as the toll of the bell which called the faithful to worship. Only God could forgive sins, could and did, washing them away in the agonal blood of His crucified Son, but that did not change the responsibility of His children to atone for those sins (and even their simple errors of judgement) whenever possible. Atonement was powerful; it was the lock on the door you closed against the past.

I fell asleep thinking of piney-woods atonement, and Eduard Delacroix on fire as he rode the lightning, and Melinda Moores, and my big boy with the endlessly weeping eyes. These thoughts twisted their way into a dream. In it, John Coffey was sitting on a riverbank and bawling his inarticulate mooncalf's grief up at the early-summer sky while on the other bank a freight-train stormed endlessly toward a rusty trestle spanning the Trapingus. In the crook of each arm the black man held the body of a naked, blonde-haired girlchild. His fists, huge brown rocks at the ends of those arms, were closed. All around him crickets chirred and noseeums flocked; the day hummed with heat. In my dream I went to him, knelt before him, and took his hands. His fists relaxed and gave up their secrets. In one was a spool colored green and red and yellow. In the other was a prison guard's shoe.

"I couldn't help it," John Coffey said. "I tried to take it back, but it was too late."

And this time, in my dream, I understood him.

8

At nine o'clock the next morning, while I was having a third cup of coffee in the kitchen (my wife said nothing, but I could see disapproval writ large on her face when she brought it to me), the telephone rang. I went into the parlor to take it, and Central told someone that their party was holding the line. She then told me to have a birdlarky day and rang off . . . presumably. With Central, you could never quite tell for sure.

Hal Moores's voice shocked me. Wavery and hoarse, it sounded like the voice of an octogenarian. It occurred to me that it was good that things had gone all right with Curtis Anderson in the tunnel last night, good that he felt about the same as we did about Percy, because this man I was talking to would very likely never work another day at Cold Mountain.

"Paul, I understand there was trouble last night. I also understand that our friend Mr. Wetmore was involved."

"A spot of trouble," I admitted, holding the

receiver tight to my ear and leaning in toward the horn, "but the job got done. That's the important thing."

"Yes. Of course."

"Can I ask who told you?" So I can tie a can to his tail? I didn't add.

"You can ask, but since it's really none of your beeswax, I think I'll keep my mouth shut on that score. But when I called my office to see if there were any messages or urgent business, I was told an interesting thing."

"Oh?"

"Yes. Seems a transferral application landed in my basket. Percy Wetmore wants to go to Briar Ridge as soon as possible. Must have filled out the application even before last night's shift was over, wouldn't you think?"

"It sounds that way," I agreed.

"Ordinarily I'd let Curtis handle it, but considering the ... atmosphere on E Block just lately, I asked Hannah to run it over to me personally on her lunch hour. She has graciously agreed to do so. I'll approve it and see it's forwarded on to the state capital this afternoon. I expect you'll get a look at Percy's backside going out the door in no more than a month. Maybe less."

He expected me to be pleased with this news, and had a right to expect it. He had taken time out from tending his wife to expedite a matter that might otherwise have taken upwards of half a year, even with Percy's vaunted connections. Nevertheless, my heart sank. A month! But maybe it didn't matter much, one way or the other. It removed a perfectly natural desire to wait and put off a risky endeavor, and what I was now thinking about would be very risky indeed. Sometimes, when that's the case, it's better to jump before you can lose your nerve. If we were going to have to deal with Percy in any case (always assuming I could get the others to go along with my insanity—always assuming there was a we, in other words), it might as well be tonight.

"Paul? Are you there?" His voice lowered a little, as if he thought he was now talking to himself. "Damn, I think I lost the connection."

"No, I'm here, Hal. That's great news."

"Yes," he agreed, and I was again struck by how old he sounded. How *papery*, somehow. "Oh, I know what you're thinking."

No, you don't, Warden, I thought. Never in a million years could you know what I'm thinking.

"You're thinking that our young friend will still be around for the Coffey execution. That's probably true—Coffey will go well before Thanksgiving, I imagine—but you can put him back in the switch room. No one will object. Including him, I should think."

"I'll do that," I said. "Hal, how's Melinda?"

There was a long pause—so long I might have thought I'd lost him, except for the sound of his breathing. When he spoke this time, it was in a much lower tone of voice. "She's sinking," he said.

Sinking. That chilly word the old-timers used not

to describe a person who was dying, exactly, but one who had begun to uncouple from living.

"The headaches seem a little better ... for now, anyway ... but she can't walk without help, she can't pick things up, she loses control of her water while she sleeps ..." There was another pause, and then, in an even lower voice, Hal said something that sounded like "She wears."

"Wears what, Hal?" I asked, frowning. My wife had come into the parlor doorway. She stood there wiping her hands on a dishtowel and looking at me.

"No," he said in a voice that seemed to waver between anger and tears. "She *swears*."

"Oh." I still didn't know what he meant, but had no intention of pursuing it. I didn't have to; he did it for me.

"She'll be all right, perfectly normal, talking about her flower-garden or a dress she saw in the catalogue, or maybe about how she heard Roosevelt on the radio and how wonderful he sounds, and then, all at once, she'll start to say the most awful things, the most awful ... words. She doesn't raise her voice. It would almost be better if she did, I think, because then ... you see, *then* ..."

"She wouldn't sound so much like herself."

"That's it," he said gratefully. "But to hear her saying those awful gutter-language things in her sweet voice ... pardon me, Paul." His voice trailed away and I heard him noisily clearing his throat. Then he came back, sounding a little stronger but just as distressed. "She wants to have Pastor Donaldson over, and I know he's a comfort to her, but how can I ask him? Suppose that he's sitting there, reading Scripture with her, and she calls him a foul name? She could; she called me one last night. She said, 'Hand me that *Liberty* magazine, you cocksucker, would you?' Paul, where could she have ever heard such language? How could she know those words?"

"I don't know. Hal, are you going to be home this evening?"

When he was well and in charge of himself, not distracted by worry or grief, Hal Moores had a cutting and sarcastic facet to his personality; his subordinates feared that side of him even more than his anger or his contempt, I think. His sarcasm, usually impatient and often harsh, could sting like acid. A little of that now splashed on me. It was unexpected, but on the whole I was glad to hear it. All the fight hadn't gone out of him after all, it seemed.

"No," he said, "I'm taking Melinda out square-dancing. We're going to do si-do, allemand left, and then tell the fiddler he's a rooster-dick mother-fucker."

I clapped my hand over my mouth to keep from laughing. Mercifully, it was an urge that passed in a hurry.

"I'm sorry," he said. "I haven't been getting much sleep lately. It's made me grouchy. Of course we're going to be home. Why do you ask?"

"It doesn't matter, I guess," I said.

"You weren't thinking of coming by, were you?

Because if you were on last night, you'll be on tonight. Unless you've switched with somebody?"

"No, I haven't switched," I said. "I'm on tonight."

"It wouldn't be a good idea, anyway. Not the way
she is right now."

"Maybe not. Thanks for your news."

"You're welcome. Pray for my Melinda, Paul."

I said I would, thinking that I might do quite a bit
more than pray. God helps those who help themselves, as they say in The Church of Praise Jesus, The
Lord Is Mighty. I hung up and looked at Janice.

"How's Melly?" she asked.

"Not good." I told her what Hal had told me, including the part about the swearing, although I left
out cocksucker and rooster-dick motherfucker. I finished with Hal's word, *sinking*, and Jan nodded
sadly. Then she took a closer look at me.

"What are you thinking about? You're thinking
about *something*, probably no good. It's in your face."

Lying was out of the question; it wasn't the way
we were with each other. I just told her it was best
she not know, at least for the time being.

"Is it . . . could it get you in trouble?" She didn't
sound particularly alarmed at the idea—more inter-
ested than anything—which is one of the things I
have always loved about her.

"Maybe," I said.

"Is it a good thing?"

"Maybe," I repeated. I was standing there, still
turning the phone's crank idly with one finger, while

I held down the connecting points with a finger of my other hand.

"Would you like me to leave you alone while you use the telephone?" she asked. "Be a good little woman and butt out? Do some dishes? Knit some booties?"

I nodded. "That's not the way I'd put it, but—"

"Are we having extras for lunch, Paul?"

"I hope so," I said.

9

I got Brutal and Dean right away, because both of them were on the exchange. Harry wasn't, not then, at least, but I had the number of his closest neighbor who was. Harry called me back about twenty minutes later, highly embarrassed at having to reverse the charges and sputtering promises to "pay his share" when our next bill came. I told him we'd count those chickens when they hatched; in the meantime, could he come over to my place for lunch? Brutal and Dean would be here, and Janice had promised to put out some of her famous slaw ... not to mention her even more famous apple pie.

"Lunch just for the hell of it?" Harry sounded skeptical.

I admitted I had something I wanted to talk to them about, but it was best not gone into, even lightly, over the phone. Harry agreed to come. I dropped the receiver onto the prongs, went to the window, and looked out thoughtfully. Although we'd had the late shift, I hadn't wakened either Brutal or Dean, and Harry hadn't sounded like a fellow freshly turned out of dreamland, either. It seemed that I wasn't the only one having problems with what had happened last night, and considering the craziness I had in mind, that was probably good.

Brutal, who lived closest to me, arrived at quarter past eleven. Dean showed up fifteen minutes later, and Harry—already dressed for work—about fifteen minutes after Dean. Janice served us cold beef sandwiches, slaw, and iced tea in the kitchen. Only a day before, we would have had it out on the side porch and been glad of a breeze, but the temperature had dropped a good fifteen degrees since the thunderstorm, and a keen-edged wind was snuffling down from the ridges.

"You're welcome to sit down with us," I told my wife.

She shook her head. "I don't think I want to know what you're up to—I'll worry less if I'm in the dark. I'll have a bite in the parlor. I'm visiting with Miss Jane Austen this week, and she's very good company."

"Who's Jane Austen?" Harry asked when she had left. "Your side or Janices's, Paul? A cousin? Is she pretty?"

"She's a writer, you nit," Brutal told him. "Been dead practically since Betsy Ross basted the stars on the first flag."

"Oh." Harry looked embarrassed. "I'm not much of a reader. Radio manuals, mostly."

"What's on your mind, Paul?" Dean asked.

"John Coffey and Mr. Jingles, to start with." They

looked surprised, which I had expected—they'd been thinking I wanted to discuss either Delacroix or Percy. Maybe both. I looked at Dean and Harry. "The thing with Mr. Jingles—what Coffey did—happened pretty fast. I don't know if you got there in time to see how broken up the mouse was or not."

Dean shook his head. "I saw the blood on the floor, though."

I turned to Brutal.

"That son of a bitch Percy crushed it," he said simply. "It should have died, but it didn't. Coffey did something to it. Healed it somehow. I know how that sounds, but I saw it with my own eyes."

I said: "He healed me, as well, and I didn't just see it, I *felt* it." I told them about my urinary infection—how it had come back, how bad it had been (I pointed through the window at the woodpile I'd had to hold onto the morning the pain drove me to my knees), and how it had gone away completely after Coffey touched me. And stayed away.

It didn't take long to tell. When I was done, they sat and thought about it awhile, chewing on their sandwiches as they did. Then Dean said, "Black things came out of his mouth. Like bugs."

"That's right," Harry agreed. "They were black to start with, anyway. Then they turned white and disappeared." He looked around, considering. "It's like I damned near forgot the whole thing until you brought it up, Paul. Ain't that funny?"

"Nothing funny or strange about it," Brutal said. "I think that's what people most always do with the stuff they can't make out—just forget it. Doesn't do a person much good to remember stuff that doesn't make any sense. What about it, Paul? Were there bugs when he fixed you?"

"Yes. I think they're the sickness ... the pain ... the hurt. He takes it in, then lets it out into the open air again."

"Where it dies," Harry said.

I shrugged. I didn't know if it died or not, wasn't sure it even mattered.

"Did he suck it out of you?" Brutal asked. "He looked like he was sucking it right out of the mouse. The hurt. The ... you know. The death."

"No," I said. "He just touched me. And I felt it. A kind of jolt, like electricity only not painful. But I wasn't dying, only hurting."

Brutal nodded. "The touch and the breath. Just like you hear those backwoods gospel-shouters going on about."

"Praise Jesus, the Lord is mighty," I said.

"I dunno if Jesus comes into it," Brutal said, "but it seems to me like John Coffey is one mighty man."

"All right," Dean said. "If you say all this happened, I guess I believe it. God works in mysterious ways His wonders to perform. But what's it got to do with us?"

Well, that was the big question, wasn't it? I took in a deep breath and told them what I wanted to do. They listened, dumbfounded. Even Brutal, who liked to read those magazines with the stories about little green men from space, looked dumbfounded. There was a longer silence when I finished this time, and no one chewing any sandwiches.

At last, in a gentle and reasonable voice, Brutus Howell said: "We'd lose our jobs if we were caught, Paul, and we'd be very goddam lucky if that was all that happened. We'd probably end up over in A Block as guests of the state, making wallets and showering in pairs."

"Yes," I said. "That could happen."

"I can understand how you feel, a little," he went on. "You know Moores better than us—he's your friend as well as the big boss—and I know you think a lot of his wife . . ."

"She's the sweetest woman you could ever hope to meet," I said, "and she means the world to him '

"But we don't know her the way you and Janice do," Brutal said. "Do we, Paul?"

"You'd like her if you did," I said. "At least, you'd like her if you'd met her before this thing got its claws into her. She does a lot of community things, she's a good friend, and she's religious. More than that, she's funny. Used to be, anyway. She could tell you things that'd make you laugh until the tears rolled down your cheeks. But none of those things are the reason I want to help save her, if she can be saved. What's happening to her is an *offense*, goddammit, an *offense*. To the eyes and the ears and the heart."

"Very noble, but I doubt like hell if that's what put this bee in your bonnet," Brutal said. "I think it's what happened to Del. You want to balance it off somehow."

And he was right. Of course he was. I knew Melinda Moores better than the others did, but maybe not, in the end, well enough to ask them to risk their jobs for her . . . and possibly their freedom, as well. Or my own job and freedom, for that matter. I had two children, and the last thing on God's earth that I wanted my wife to have to do was to write them the news that their father was going on trial for . . . well, what would it be? I didn't know for sure. Aiding and abetting an escape attempt seemed the most likely.

But the death of Eduard Delacroix had been the ugliest, foulest thing I had ever seen in my life—not just my working life but my whole, entire life—and I had been a party to it. We had *all* been a party to it, because we had allowed Percy Wetmore to stay even after we knew he was horribly unfit to work in a place like E Block. We had played the game. Even Warden Moores had been a party to it. "His nuts are going to cook whether Wetmore's on the team or not," he had said, and maybe that was well enough, considering what the little Frenchman had done, but in the end Percy had done a lot more than cook Del's nuts; he had blown the little man's eyeballs right out of their sockets and set his damned face on fire. And why? Because Del was a murderer half a dozen times over? No. Because Percy had wet his pants and the little Cajun had had the temerity to laugh at him. We'd been part of a monstrous act, and Percy was going to get away with it. Off to Briar Ridge he would go, happy as a clam at high tide, and there he would have a whole asylum filled with lunatics to practice his cruelties upon. There was nothing we could do about that, but perhaps it was not too late to wash some of the muck off our own hands.

"In my church they call it atonement instead of balancing," I said, "but I guess it comes to the same thing."

"Do you really think Coffey *could* save her?" Dean asked in a soft, awed voice. "Just . . . what? . . . suck that brain tumor out of her head? Like it was a . . . a peach-pit?"

"I think he could. It's not for sure, of course, but after what he did to me . . . and to Mr. Jingles . . ."

"That mouse was seriously busted up, all right," Brutal said.

"But *would* he do it?" Harry mused. "*Would* he?"

"If he can, he will," I said.

"Why? Coffey doesn't even know her!"

"Because it's what he does. It's what God made him for."

Brutal made a show of looking around, reminding us all that someone was missing. "What about Percy? You think he's just gonna let this go down?" he asked, and so I told them what I had in mind for Percy. By the time I finished, Harry and Dean were looking at me in amazement, and a reluctant grin of admiration had dawned on Brutal's face.

"Pretty audacious, Brother Paul!" he said. "Fair takes my breath away!"

"But wouldn't it be the bee's knees!" Dean almost whispered, then laughed aloud and clapped his hands like a child. "I mean, voh-doh-dee-oh-doh and twenty-three-skidoo!" You want to remember that Dean had a special interest in the part of my plan that involved Percy—Percy could have gotten Dean killed, after all, freezing up the way he had.

"Yeah, but what about after?" Harry said. He sounded gloomy, but his eyes gave him away; they were sparkling, the eyes of a man who wants to be convinced. "What then?"

"They say dead men tell no tales," Brutal rumbled, and I took a quick look at him to make sure he was joking.

"I think he'll keep his mouth shut," I said.

"Really?" Dean looked skeptical. He took off his glasses and began to polish them. "Convince me."

"First, he won't know what really happened—he's going to judge us by himself and think it was just a prank. Second—and more important—*he'll be afraid to say anything*. That's what I'm really counting on. We tell him that if he starts writing letters and making phone calls, *we* start writing letters and making phone calls."

"About the execution," Harry said.

"And about the way he froze when Wharton attacked Dean," Brutal said. "I think people finding out about that is what Percy Wetmore's really afraid of." He nodded slowly and thoughtfully. "It could work. But Paul ... wouldn't it make more sense to bring Mrs. Moores to Coffey than Coffey to Mrs.

Moores? We could take care of Percy pretty much the way you laid it out, then bring her in through the tunnel instead of taking Coffey out that way."

I shook my head. "Never happen. Not in a million years."

"Because of Warden Moores?"

"That's right. He's so hardheaded he makes old Doubting Thomas look like Joan of Arc. If we bring Coffey to his house, I think we can surprise him into at least letting Coffey make the try. Otherwise . . ."

"What were you thinking about using for a vehicle?" Brutal asked.

"My first thought was the stagecoach," I said, "but we'd never get it out of the yard without being noticed, and everyone within a twenty-mile radius knows what it looks like, anyway. I guess maybe we can use my Ford."

"Guess again," Dean said, popping his specs back onto his nose. "You couldn't get John Coffey into your car if you stripped him naked, covered him with lard, and used a shoehorn. You're so used to looking at him that you've forgotten how big he is."

I had no reply to that. Most of my attention that morning had been focused on the problem of Percy—and the lesser but not inconsiderable problem of Wild Bill Wharton. Now I realized that transportation wasn't going to be as simple as I had hoped.

Harry Terwilliger picked up the remains of his second sandwich, looked at it for a second, then put it down again. "If we was to actually do this crazy thing," he said, "I guess we could use my pickup truck. Sit him in the back of that. Wouldn't be no-body much on the roads at that hour. We're talking about well after midnight, ain't we?"

"Yes," I said.

"You guys're forgetting one thing," Dean said. "I know Coffey's been pretty quiet ever since he came on the block, doesn't do much but lay there on his bunk and leak from the eyes, but he's a *murderer*. Also, he's *huge*. If he decided he wanted to escape out of the back of Harry's truck, the only way we could stop him would be to shoot him dead. And a guy like that would take a lot of killing, even with a .45. Suppose we weren't able to put him down? And suppose he killed someone else? I'd hate losing my job, and I'd hate going to jail—I got a wife and kids depending on me to put bread in their mouths—but I don't think I'd hate either of those things near as much as having another dead little girl on my con-science."

"That won't happen," I said.

"How in God's name can you be so sure of that?"

I didn't answer. I didn't know just how to begin. I had known this would come up, of course I did, but I still didn't know how to start telling them what I knew. Brutal helped me.

"You don't think he did it, do you, Paul?" He looked incredulous. "You think that big lug is inno-cent."

"I'm positive he's innocent," I said.

"How in the name of Jesus *can* you be?"

"There are two things," I said. "One of them is my shoe." I leaned forward over the table and began talking.

To Be Continued

Welcome to the loneliest highway,
and the deadliest ...

DESPERATION

by Stephen King

Just off Route 50 in Nevada lies the small mining town of Desperation, where a local cop has suddenly turned anything but lawman. His victims were the lucky ones. But for a small group of survivors, desperation is no longer just the name of a town—it's a state of mind. And it will take an extraordinary young boy to lead them through a living nightmare.

Coming in September 1996
A Viking Hardcover Book

*The suburbs have never been
more terrifying ...*

THE REGULATORS

by Richard Bachman

It's a summer afternoon in Wentworth, Ohio,
and on Poplar Street, everything's normal ...
except for the red van idling just up the hill.
Soon it will begin to roll, and the madness
will begin. And by the time night falls, the
surviving residents will find themselves in another world, one where anything is possible
... and where The Regulators are on their
way.

Coming in September 1996
A Dutton Hardcover Book

Escaping a madman was the easy part . . .

ROSE MADDER
by Stephen king

Rose Daniels saw the single drop of blood on the bed sheet—and knew she must escape from her macabre marriage before it was too late. But tracking Rose is her sadistic cop of a husband, Norman, a terrifying monster and a savage brute. The only place Rose has found to hide could be the most dangerous of all . . .

**Available Now
A Signet Paperback**

Return to a world of extraordinary vision . . .

THE DARK TOWER IV
Wizard and Glass
by Stephen King

The epic journey of Roland the Gunslinger continues in this long-awaited fourth volume. Find out what happens after Roland and his friends Susannah and Eddie begin their amazing ride out of the city and into the realms of a world still unexplored . . .

**Available Summer 1997
A Plume Trade Paperback**

Win an Autographed Stephen King Library!

Enter
THE GREEN MILE Contest!

6 winners per month will receive an autographed GREEN MILE manuscript (36 winners total). All winners are then eligible for the Grand Prize— an autographed Stephen King library!

See reverse side for details.

Name _____

Address _____

City _____

State_____ Zip Code _____

To enter:

1. Answer the following question:

   Brad Dolan, the orderly at Georgia Pines, reminds the narrator of Percy Wetmore. What similarities do the two of them share?

2. Write your answer on a separate piece of paper (in 50 words or less)

3. Mail to: **THE GREEN MILE PART 4 CONTEST, P.O. Box 9035, Medford, NY, 11763**

OFFICIAL RULES

1. To enter, hand print your name and complete address on the official entry form (original, photocopy, or a plain piece of paper). Then, on a separate piece of paper (no larger than 8-1/2" x 11") in 50 words or less, hand-printed or typed, complete the following statement:

Brad Dolan, the orderly at Georgia Pines, reminds the narrator of Percy Wetmore. What similarities do the two of them share?

Staple your statement to your entry form and mail to: THE GREEN MILE PART 4 CONTEST, P.O. Box 9035, Medford, NY 11763. Entries must be received by August 30, 1996, to be eligible. Not responsible for late, lost, misdirected mail or printing errors.

2. All entries will be judged by Marden-Kane, Inc., an independent judging organization in conjunction with Penguin USA based upon the following criteria: Originality 35%, Content 35%, Sincerity 20%, and Clarity 10%. By entering this contest, entrants accept and agree to be bound to these rules and the decisions of the judges which shall be final and binding. All entries become the property of the sponsor and will not be acknowledged or returned. Each entry must be the original work of the entrant. Winners will be notified by mail and may be required to execute an affidavit of eligibility and release which must be returned within 14 days of notification or an alternate winner will be selected.

3. PRIZES: Six (6) winners for each part of THE GREEN MILE will receive a manuscript of THE GREEN MILE autographed by Stephen King (36 winners total). Approximate retail value: $100.00. All winners in subsequent GREEN MILE contests are eligible to win a Grand Prize of an autographed Stephen King library. Approximate retail value: $1000.00. Grand Prize will be awarded after November 29, 1996, based upon criteria outlined above.

4. Contest open to residents of the United States and Canada 18 years of age and older, except employees and the immediate families of Penguin USA, its affiliates, subsidiaries, advertising agencies, and Marden-Kane, Inc. Void in FL, VT, MD, AZ, the Province of Quebec, and wherever else prohibited by law. All Federal, State, Local, and Provincial laws apply. Taxes, if any, are the sole responsibility of the prize winners. If winners are Canadian, he/she will be required to answer an arithmetical skill testing question administered by mail. Winners consent to the use of their name and/or photos or likeness for advertising purposes without additional compensation (except where prohibited).

5. For the names of the major prize winners, send a self-addressed, stamped envelope after August 30, 1996, to: THE GREEN MILE CONTEST WINNER, P.O. Box 5000, Manhasset, NY, 11030.

Ⓓ Signet
Penguin USA • Mass Market